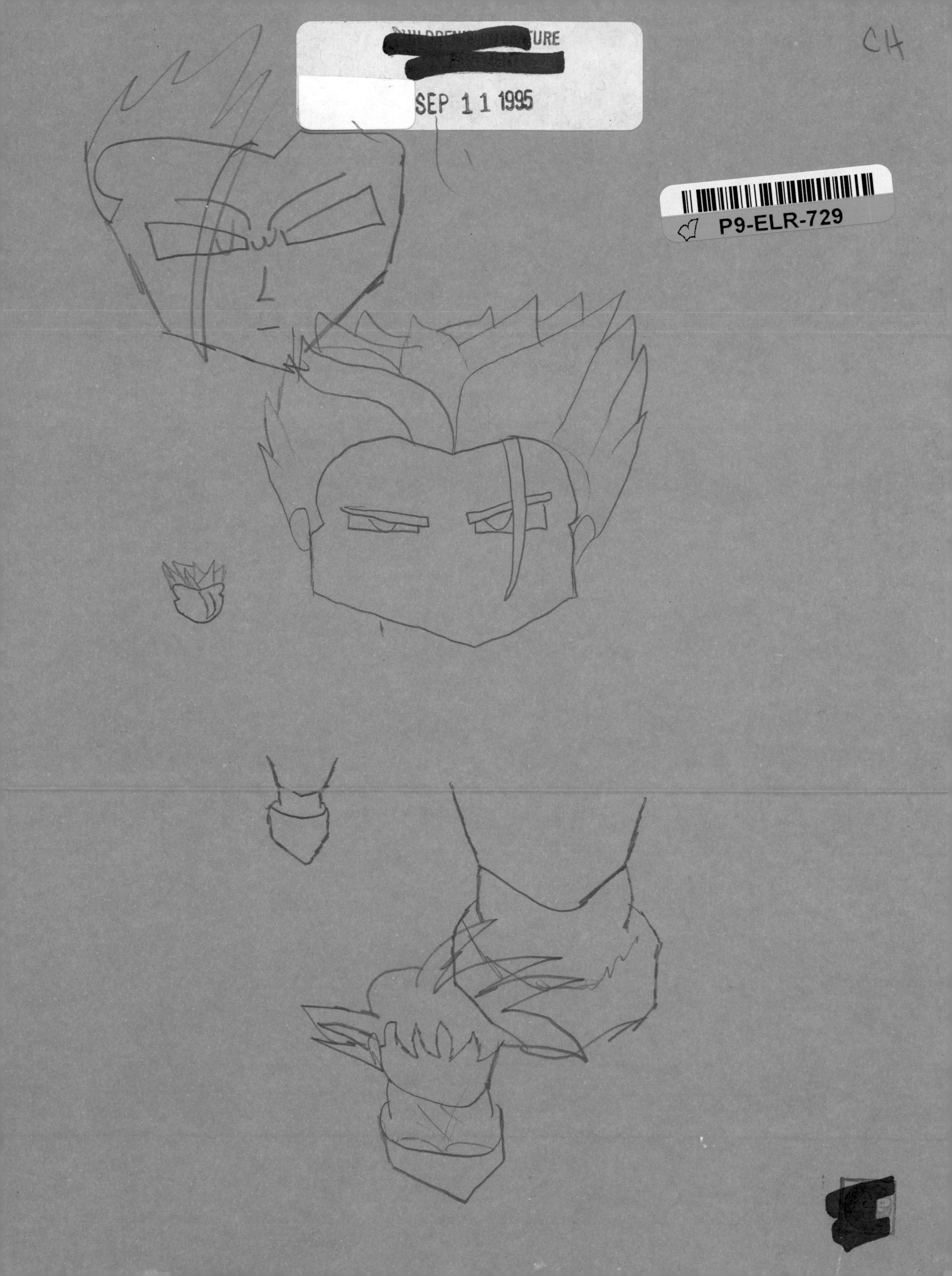
CH
SEP 1 1 1995
P9-ELR-729

How the Sky's Housekeeper Wore Her SCARVES

by PATRICIA HOOPER

Collages by SUSAN L. ROTH

Little, Brown and Company
Boston New York Toronto London

First Edition

Library of Congress Cataloging-in-Publication Data
Hooper, Patricia, 1941–
How the sky's housekeeper wore her scarves / by Patricia Hooper ; collages by Susan L. Roth — 1st ed.
p. cm.
Summary: Explains why the rainbow comes out when the sun shines through the rain.
ISBN 0-316-37255-2
[1. Rainbow — Fiction.] I. Roth, Susan L., ill. II. Title.
PZ7.H7693Sk 1995
[E] — dc20

10 9 8 7 6 5 4 3 2 1

NIL

Published simultaneously in Canada by Little, Brown & Company (Canada) Limited

Printed in Italy

The collages for this book were created with papers, fabrics, metallic foils, and other materials (such as unspun flax, used for the old woman's hair) collected by the illustrator from places all over the universe.

For Mitzi Alvin and Gay Rubin

P. H.

For Steph — thank you and love

S. L. R.

In a house at the back of the wind lived an old woman who kept seven colorful scarves tucked in a box.

On Mondays she wore the **red** one when she went to polish the sun.

On Tuesdays she wore the **orange** one when she went to dust off the moon.

On Wednesdays she wore the yellow one when she went to straighten the stars.

On Thursdays she wore the **green** one when she went to wind up the comets.

On Fridays she wore the **blue** one when she went to sweep off the Milky Way.

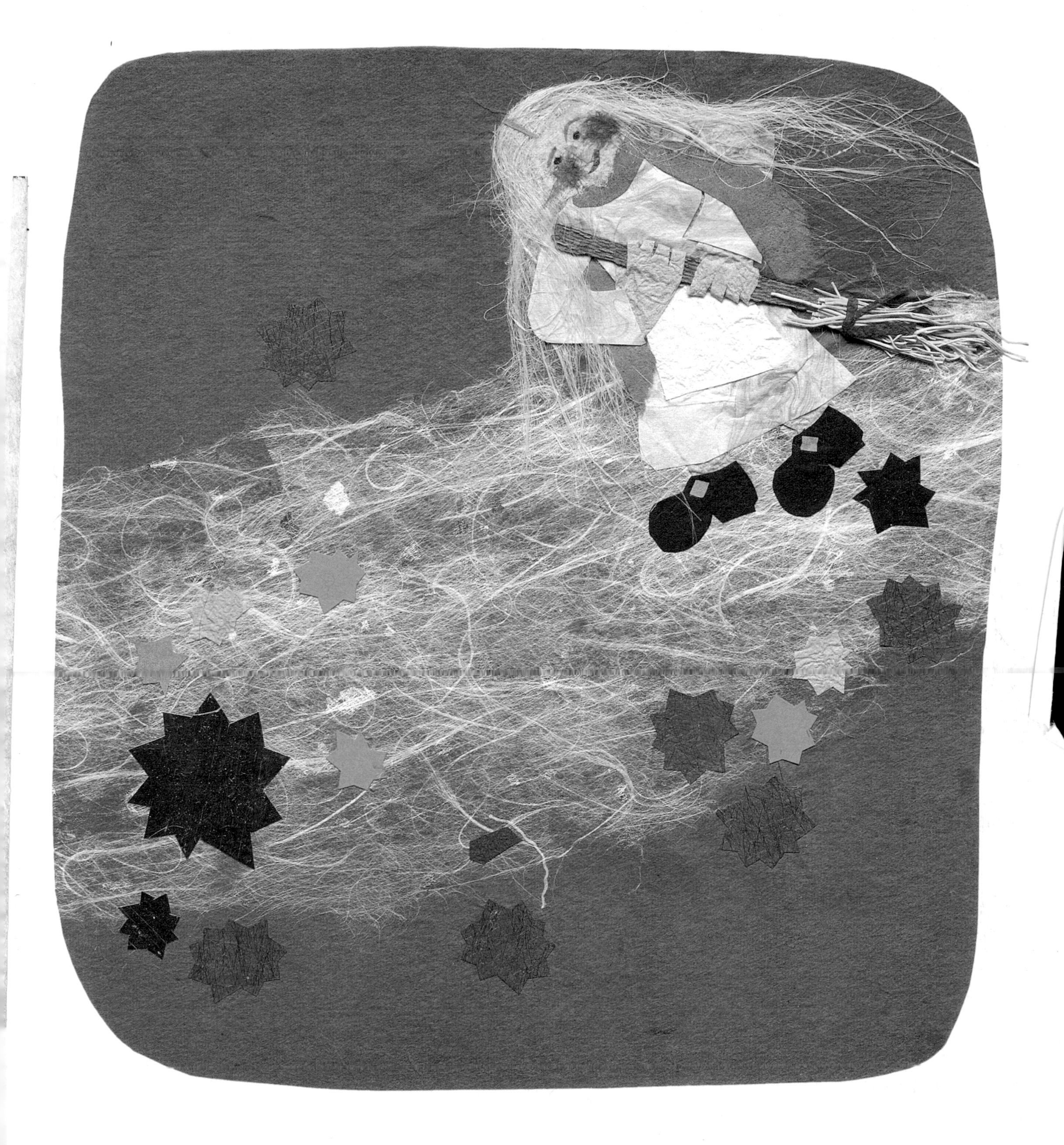

On Saturdays she wore the **indigo** one when she went with her bucket of soap suds to scrub the planets.

And on Sundays she wore the **violet** one when she sat with her sewing basket and mended clouds.

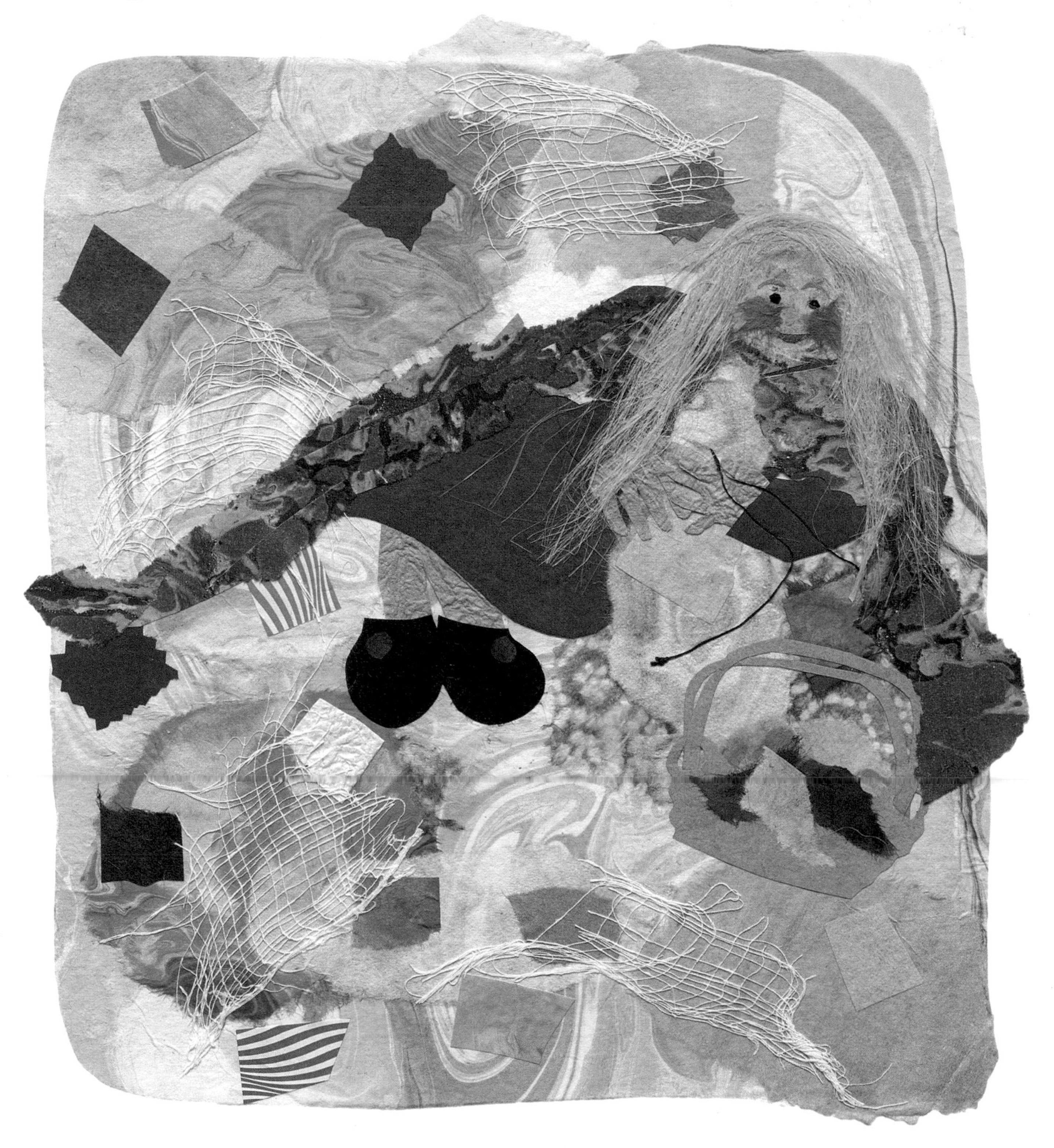

She had lived longer than even the sun could remember, and had always worn one of her scarves when she did her work.

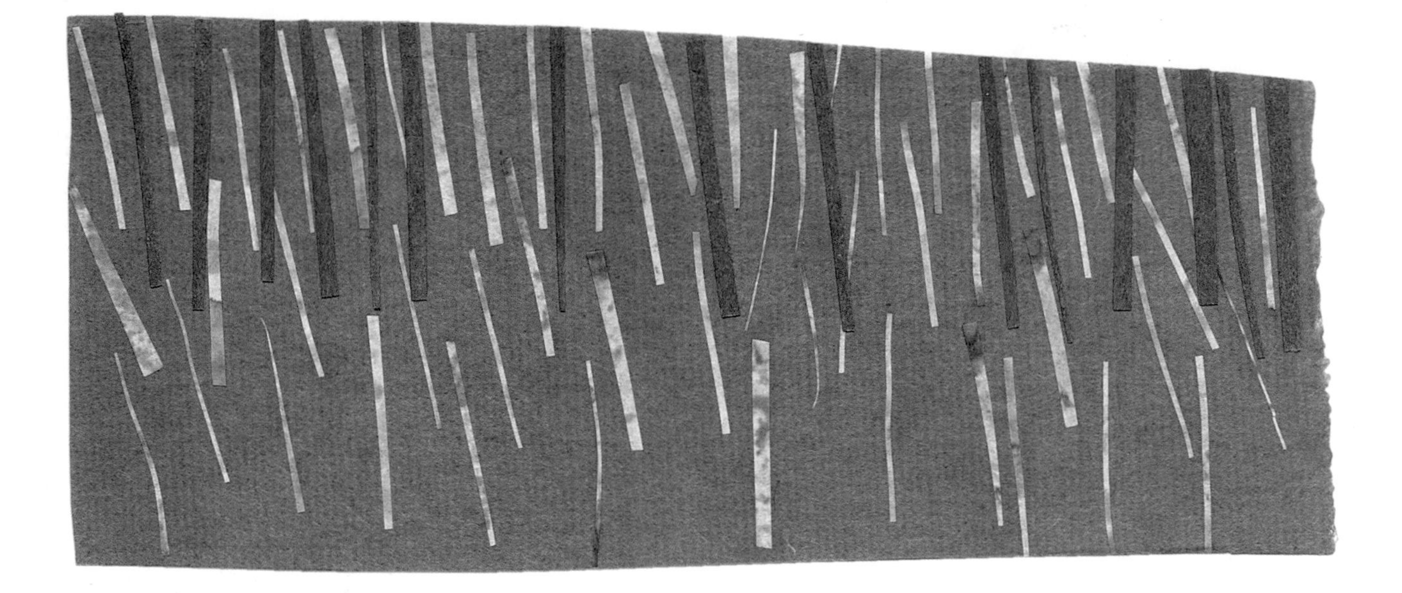

One morning, as the old woman was sorting the wind's laundry, the rain knocked at her window.

"What is it you want?" asked the old woman, pressing her ear to the glass. She did not want to let the rain in if she could help it.

"I want things to be different," the rain moaned. "The sun is so cheerful, just seeing him makes me happy. But whenever he sees me coming, he disappears."

"That's how the sun is," said the old woman. "He loves his own brightness and hates to see anything dreary. But why have you come to me?"

"I've seen you wearing your scarves," the rain told her. "Sometimes I think it's the evening sun, but it's only your **red** or **orange** scarf glowing like sunset.

"Sometimes I think it's the morning sun, but it's only your yellow scarf sparkling like sunrise.

"And sometimes, in your **green, blue, indigo,** or **violet** scarf, you look like the sun shining on fields or water. But one thing is certain, I always feel much better if I can see you."

The old woman was flattered. But the rain, who was trickling in and forming a puddle, went on talking.

"I've seen you only on sunny days, when I have to stay in my bedroom. Since your scarves are so much like sunlight, I want you to come out when I do, to cheer me up."

This startled the old woman, for she feared getting lost in the rain and always delayed her trips until it was sunny.

"Let me talk to the sun first," she suggested. "Come back after he's polished, and maybe I'll have an answer."

That afternoon the old woman put on her **red** scarf and went to polish the sun. As the sun was particular about looking his best, he was always very happy to have her visit.

"I have a favor to ask," ventured the old woman.

"Certainly," said the sun, admiring his polished face as it shone back from the ocean. "Anything you want!" It had been a long time since anyone had asked the sun for a favor.

"I want you to shine when it rains."

The sun stared disbelievingly at the old woman, for he hated to see how the rain misted his brilliance, and he hid whenever it rained, to avoid the sight.

"What a terrible thought!" cried the sun, growing more fiery. "I should have said, 'Anything you want but *that!*'" And he wailed so loudly that even the moon, who was visiting China, heard him.

The old woman felt frightened. "Very well," she said quickly. "Forget that I ever asked. I shall have to try to cheer up the rain myself." And she went home.

At home, however, she noticed the rain coming.

"Oh, dear, what shall I do?" the old woman said to herself. "He wants me to walk through the sky when the sun is hiding. But suppose I should lose my way?"

And because she knew her decision would disappoint him, she closed her curtain and crept under the table.

I'll come out tomorrow, she thought when the rain called her.

But although the rain tapped for days at her kitchen window, she could not summon the courage to go out.

In fact, the old woman was so busy avoiding the rain, she completely neglected her errands.

How dusty the moon is! the stars thought as they came out in the evening.

How crooked the stars are! thought the moon as she faded the next morning.

And the comets said sadly, "How can we chase each other? Not one of us has budged from his place for hours!"

And so it went. The Milky Way was covered with tracks and cobwebs. The planets, in need of scrubbing, were drab as stones.

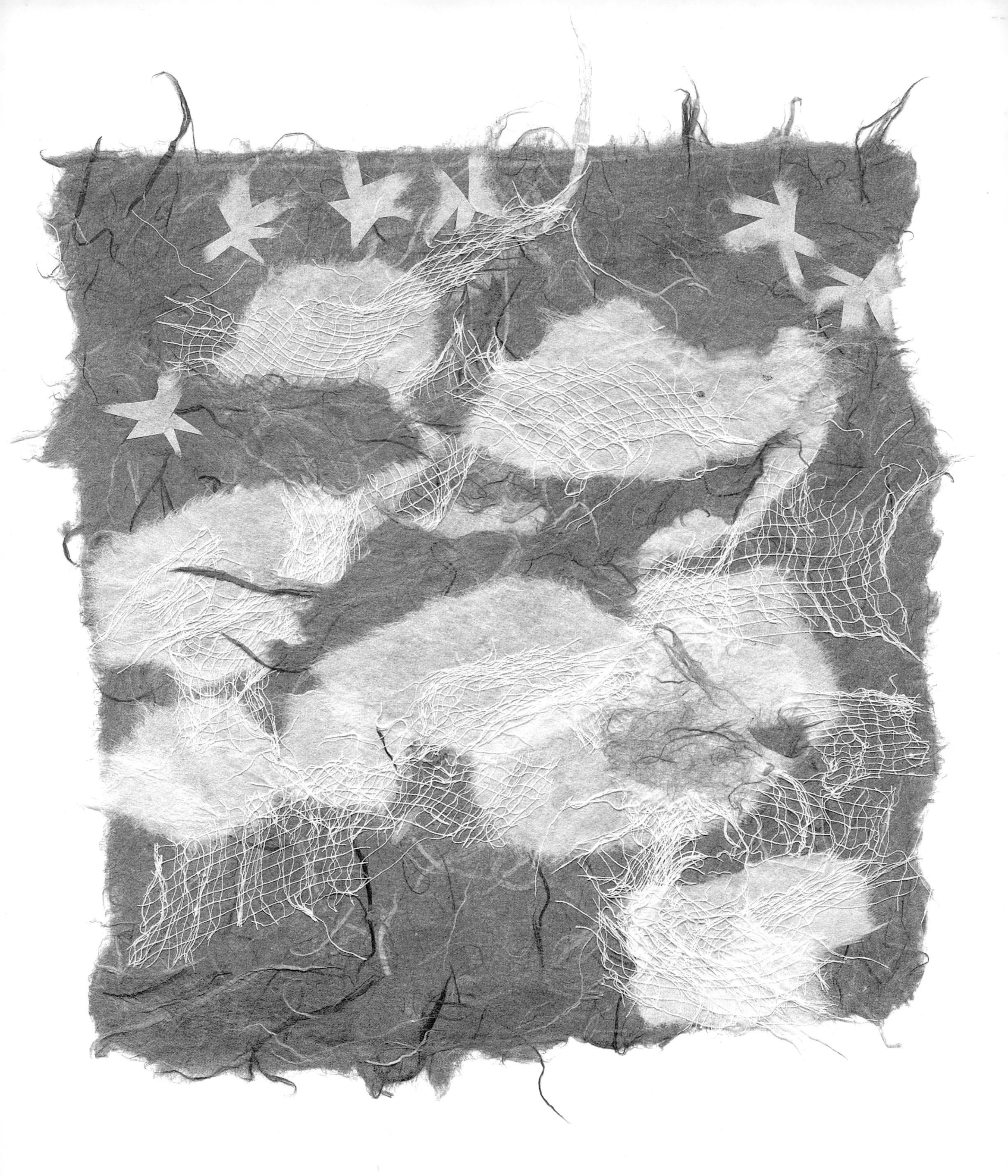

Even the clouds drifted in rags and tatters.

Finally the sun stole a glance at himself in the ocean. But to his surprise, his unpolished face was so dull he could hardly find it.

"Old woman," he called. "Come back! I NEED POLISHING!"

When the old woman heard him, she crept out of hiding and peeked through a hole in her curtain.

"Oh, dear, what have I done?" she cried. "All week I've neglected my errands, and now I must do them all in spite of the weather."

And because she had so much to do in a single day, she quickly put on all of her scarves at once.

"HURRY!" the sun called. And although it was still raining, he shone as much as he could so the old woman could find him.

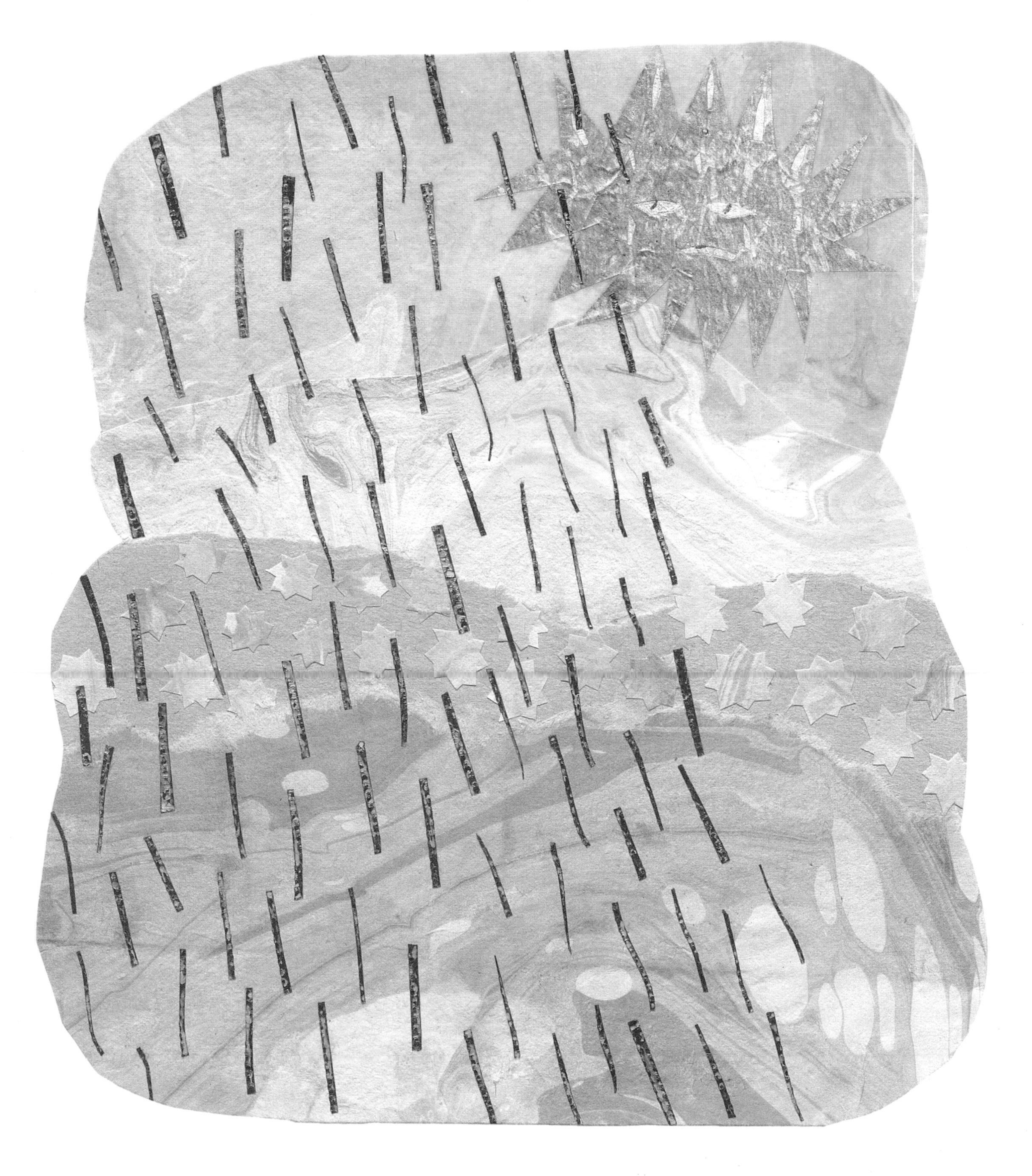

To avoid getting lost in the rain, the old woman tied one end of each of her scarves to the fence post, marking the way back. Then she climbed into the heavens. As she went, she dusted and straightened and wound and swept and scrubbed and mended. And when she had polished the sun, she sat down on the horizon.

"It's time to find my way back," the old woman said to herself. "Thank goodness I tied the ends of my scarves to the fence post."

But just as she started to follow her scarves home, gathering them up as she went and tucking them into her apron, the rain called to her.

"Old woman, look at the sky!" he cried.

When the old woman looked up, she cried out with pleasure. For there were the rain falling in the east and the sun shining in the west, and there were her scarves, shimmering in an arc at the sky's center.

The sun was delighted and called out to the rain, "The sky never looked better! If you had not come, the old woman would never have tied all of her scarves to the fence post. And if I had not shone, they would never have seemed so bright. If the old woman will join us, I declare we must meet again whenever she asks!"

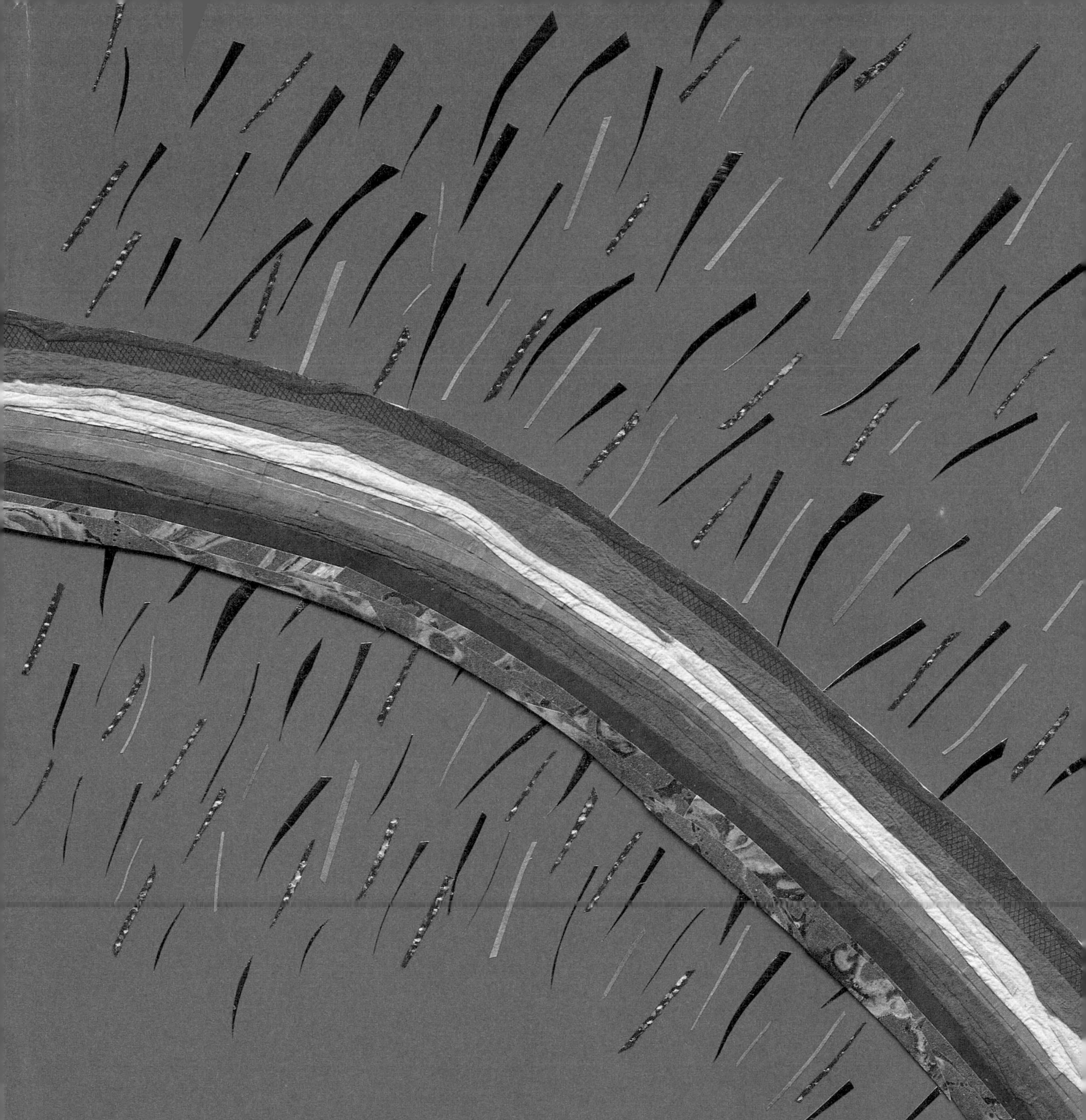

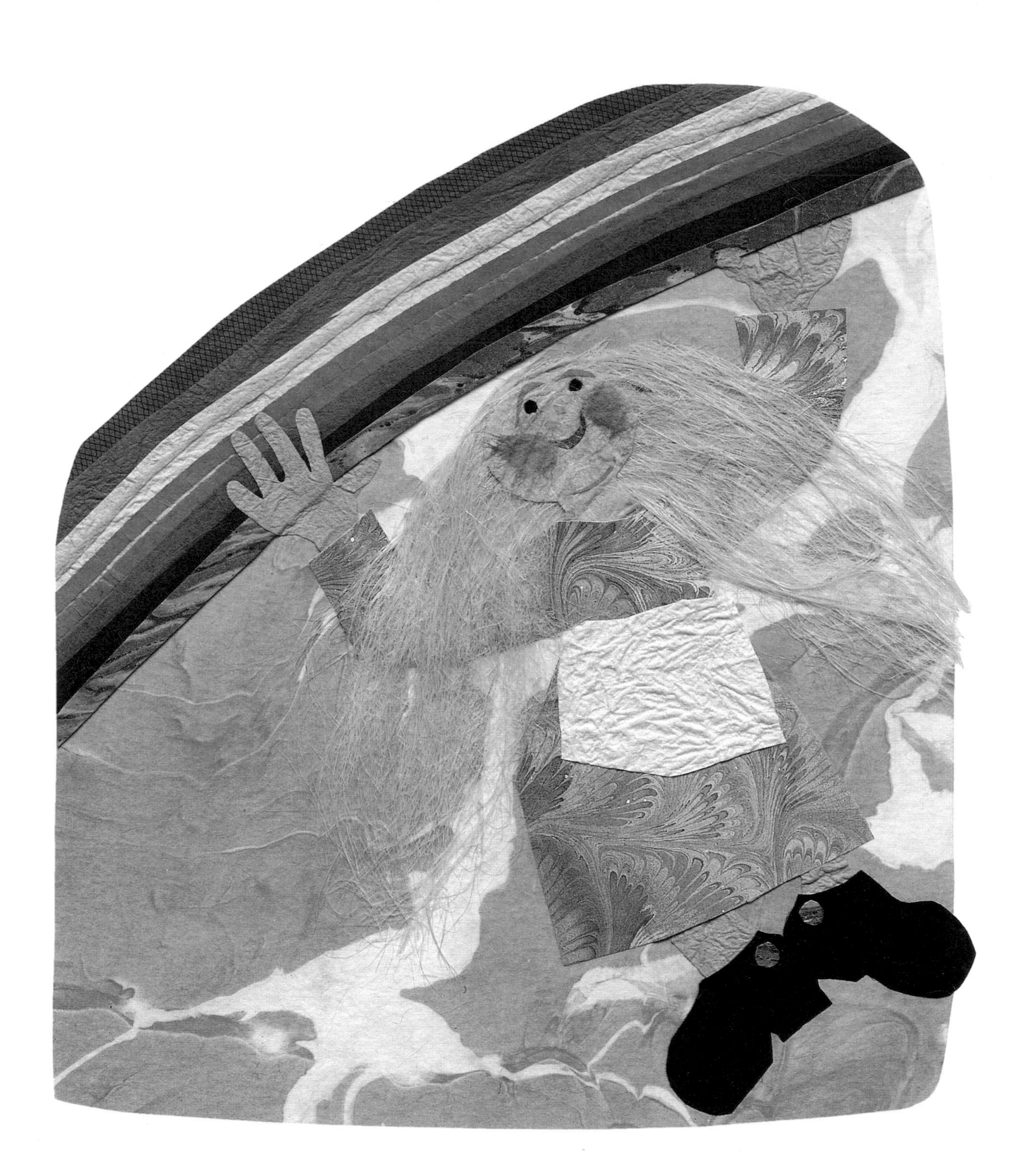

And on certain days, when the sun is shining and the rain is falling, you can see the old woman's scarves — **red, orange, yellow, green, blue, indigo,** and **violet** — stretching in an arc from one end of the sky to the other.